52
Laws
of
love

52 laws
of love

himanshu goel

Kalamos Literary Services LLP

Kalamos Literary Services LLP
Email: info@kalamos.co.in | editorial@kalamos.co.in
Published in 2020
by
Kalamos Literary Services
ISBN- 978-93-87780-60-6

Copyright © Himanshu Goel 2020
52 laws of love

Typeset in Kalamos Literary Services LLP

Dedicated to
Mom and Dad

a love that is true

1

if there can
be laws of the universe
written in the language of maths
why can't be there laws of love
written in the language of poetry.

2

it's not true love I seek
but a love that is true
the kind that's so hard
to find in this world.

3

before we become lovers
we must learn to be friends
and before we befriend
we must learn to be strangers

4

don't let me be lost
in the crowd
there'll be many
suitable suitors
but I'll mark
my heart for you.

5

I found love in
an unknown street
of an unknown town
in an abandoned lighthouse
where no ships passed by
what a fool I was thinking
I had found love
when all along
it found me.

6

they say only
fools believe
in a love that is true
and only fools dream
then we'd rather be fools
than not love and not dream

7

they say the rivers of love
have been polluted
it isn't like how it used to be
they say like the love of old
it isn't supposed to be we say
let's show them a love like
they have never seen before.

8

aren't we all chasing
those damn butterflies
that warm blanket
in the coldest of days
when we catch them
we have found our love.

9

when our words run out
and silence is the
most comfortable sound
we'll know we are ready.

10

you have been
through the fires
of hell and seen
the gates of heaven
you have soared through
the skies and slept in the deep sea
but brace yourself for you
have never felt anything like love.

11

let me warn you darling
I am a little hard
to love at first sight
but by the 52nd one
I promise
I'll make you fall for me.

12

I know you are waiting
for that perfect moment
but this time don't count
on the flowers to bloom and
don't rely on the stars to align
I know you are waiting
for that perfect moment
but don't wait too long.

13

will you fall for me
or will you fall
for the idea of me?

14

one day you
were not there
and then
I couldn't
take another day
without you.

15

but first
show me your worst
there will be plenty
of time for your best.

16

it's here, almost but
before you come to me
lock away your secrets
in a little box and throw
away the key, we won't
be needing them anymore.

17

let's take small
steps together first
the leap of faith
will come.

addicted to love

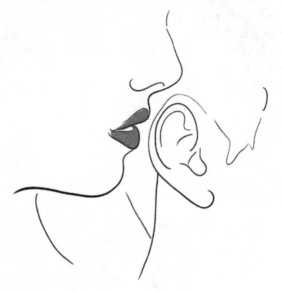

18

you must call me
by my name
not the one
that is known to
everyone but the
name that belongs to you

19

and love will come in
a thousand ways
through a thousand paths
in seasons and storms
but don't worry
there is no such thing
as a never-ending winter
and a rain that never stops.

20

when fall comes
and along with it
the inevitable fire
don't add fuel to it
for it is already bright
don't try to tame it
don't extinguish it
let it be
and when fall comes
burn alongside me

21

when snow lands
on our kingdom
prepare for war
bring your swords
and daggers
for there'll be battles
against the world and
against each other

22

in moonsoon
throw away our
coats and your
black umbrella
and let the cold
red rain seep
into our hearts

23

be wary of summer
with its warm tones
and cold hearts
sunshine for fools
and flowers for the rest
be wary of summer
after all, when did we ever
need the sun
to keep us warm?

24

don't let our
love be a cage
I have been in enough
prisons through my life already

25

when dusk escapes us and
night falls we'll fight
shadows and ghosts
of your past
together

26

don't hide your flaws from me
your subtle quirks, your dark corners
little treasures of discomfort
I love them more than you can imagine

27

these lips never
learned to move
the right way
but don't worry
a true love's kiss
is only between the souls.

28

it was easy for you to
love me even with my
quirks and flaws
but I will need your
help to learn how
to love myself

29

when we go to
the mountains
and into the woods
throw away your
camera into the lake
I won't need pictures to
remember the moments we create

30

and you saw
all the tears I carried
and you didn't run away
and you saw
all the tears
and you turned them
all into smiles.

31

while love might
satisfy our hearts
Our souls will need
art to survive.

32

whisper secrets to me
the world will never know
whisper truths to me
in this world of liars.

33

we don't have to be alone
the lonely moon, the calm sea
a birdsong and unsung lullabies
there are many allies of love.

34

just like coffee
you became
an addiction
I couldn't escape.

35

we have had our rainbows
and rains our long walks
and slow rides, but don't
put the pen down just yet
our love still has a long way to go.

the ever after

36

If the time has come
we must learn to be whole
we must learn to be friends again
and then back to strangers

37

when did our silence
meet anxiety and
when we had
so much love
how did it run dry?

38

when kisses don't heal
the wounds of
separation
and lighthouses
point in the wrong direction
what can we do when
every heartfelt gesture
turns into a song of pain?

39

love is in short supply and
doubt runs deep
tomorrow is a million miles away
and sleep takes forever to arrive.

40

love don't die easy
like a supernova
gone astray
it burns
way beyond the skin
love don't die easy
but lovers live on.

41

the days
will be long
without each other
don't let the ghosts
of love haunt us
into the night

42

if our paths part
let time cure
the kind of pain
that painkillers
can't heal

43

and things are
almost over
your friends
try but they
don't get it, do they?
but alone is a dangerous
sea where you will drown
please then swim and talk to me.

44

this tired tattered body
will eventually decay
and even the mind
can only go for so long
but in the end
our love will remain.

45

words of love that
once flew like
free birds in the spring
now take days to utter.

46

there might be more
moons and stars and shores
but don't worry darling
no other can eclipse
a love like yours.

47

the gentle rain
and merciless time
might fade our
stories away
but never
forget my name
that belongs to you
and you alone.

48

what if shakespeare
was right and
maybe our truth
was written in
stars that were crossed?

49

screw shakespeare
and screw the skies
our love, our truth
even the stars can't deny
because you are
worth the happy ending

50

this fall there was no fire
in you or me but
don't worry
I have got enough
sparks to last us seven lifetimes

51

they throw hurricanes
and tornadoes
volcanoes high
and rivers low
how can these
natural disasters
hurt us when
our love was born
in the heart of earth.

52

the ever after
wasn't happy at all'
the ever after
wasn't like the dream I had
the ever after
wasn't magic
the ever after
wasn't my fairytale
the ever after
wasn't happy at all
oh, but it was so much more.

himanshu goel

Himanshu Goel is a 24-year-old writer and blogger from Chandigarh, India. His first book Tulsi was published in 2017. His passion for storytelling made him pursue writing. His short stories and poetry have been published in several international literary collections. When not writing, he blogs on Instagram at @lighthouse_foodie. You can read more about him at himanshuwriter.com.